The Animated
MEGILLAH

A PURIM ADVENTURE
EPHRAIM SIDON   RONY OREN

Part of the series
The Animated Holydays
Series Editor - Uri Shin'ar

Published by Scopus Films (London) Ltd.
P.O.Box 565, London N6 5YS
Suite 1102, 150 Fifth Ave. New York, NY 10011

Graphic design: Chava Margol

Photography: Studio Judy & Kenny
Photographed in Frame By Frame Studios
Educational editor: Udi Lion
English translation: Debbie Silver
Print production: Ehud Oren & David Melchior
Printed by G.D.I.

Project producers: Uri Shin'ar & Jonathan Lubell
Made in Israel by Jerusalem Productions Ltd.
23 Abarbanel Street, Jerusalem 92477, Israel

U S A Distributors: J.D. Publishers
68-22 Eliot Ave.
Middle Village, N.Y. 11379 Tel. (718)456-8611

Problems at the Palace

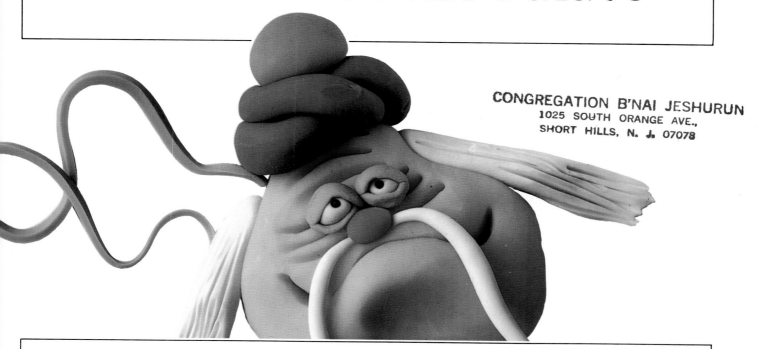

Hi. I'm Danny.

A lot of you already know me from the Haggadah and the story of my travels on Star Dreidel. For those of you who don't, here's what my passport would look like if they gave passports to kids like me:

Name:	Danny
Age:	10-1/2
Height:	4 ft., 4 in.
Weight:	68 lbs.
Eyes:	Stunning
Hair:	Depends on the sun. Sometimes red, sometimes brown.
Distinguishing marks:	One sister, Judy, age 12
Permanent address:	Kids' Room
Profession:	Child
Ambition:	To be big and famous

That's who I am, but not what I'm here to tell you about.

It all began one awful Tuesday. Judy and I were both in bad moods because we had these tough homework assignments that had to be ready by Thursday. I had to talk to an old person about something from the past and to write a report of what I heard. That's the sort of homework I really hate. Judy had to write about her favorite heroine. All the way home from school she complained that she didn't have one.

Grumbling, we came home and found Mom in the kitchen up to her elbows in flour. She explained that she was making Hamentaschen for the next day, Purim.

"Purim!" Judy and I exclaimed together. We'd forgotten! How were we going to enjoy anything, much less a holiday, with the homework that we had hanging over our heads?

While Judy complained to Mom about heroines, I went up to Grandpa Sam's bedroom.

But once in his room, I thought for a moment that he'd flipped his lid! He was wearing a wig, red lipstick, rouge . . . and one of Grandma Rebecca's dresses.

"Grandpa," I said very carefully, "why are you wearing a dress?"

"It's Purim tomorrow," he explained chuckling. "I thought I'd wear a costume, as you and Judy do, when we read the Megillah tomorrow night. When I was a little boy in Poland, only the children and the Purim players used to dress up. But why shouldn't I have some fun too? So I'm coming as Grandma."

Memories, right? I whipped out my notebook. Grandpa told me what a riot it was watching silly plays about good Mordechai and wicked Haman. He said everybody would shout and wave noisemakers —— groggers —— every time Haman was mentioned during the reading of the Megillah to block out the sound of his name, just like we do on Purim nowadays. The adults would drink schnapps.

In no time, I had a full notebook and it was time for supper.

Later that night, after we were in bed, Judy wouldn't put out the light. She was reading a book Mom had given her.

"It's the real story of Purim," she explained. "Listen to this: 'Now it came to pass in the days of Ahasuerus who reigned over one hundred and twenty and seven kingdoms, even from Ethiopia to India . . .'"

"Skip it, Judy," I said. "I'm tired. Turn out the light."

"You're just like Ahasuerus!" she shouted, throwing the book across the room at me.

"You mean, like a king?" I asked.

"No, an idiot!" she replied, and burst out laughing.

I couldn't see what was so funny.

And then someone knocked on our window.

We both froze. I looked at Judy.

"Well, open it then," I told her.

"No, you do it," she said.

"Not me! You're supposed to be the heroine around here!"

She made a face at me and was just about to get out of bed when the knock came again, much louder this time, breaking a pane of glass all over the floor. Tucking my head under the covers seemed a good idea. I couldn't resist peeking, though. When I looked, there was Judy, staring open-mouthed at this funny looking man standing in the middle of our room.

How can I describe him? He was dressed in these strange clothes. On his head was a fez with a curved top and he was wearing a silky shirt and trousers that bagged out at the ankles. He looked like an extra from some old movie.

I decided I'd better be brave, since Judy was still gaping.

"Who are you?" I demanded in my bravest voice.

The stranger didn't answer. Instead, he took off his hat. Underneath it was a scroll of paper tied with a ribbon and sealed with wax. He handed it to me. I opened it and read out loud:

I have read of your heroic deeds in the time of Antiochus and was most impressed by the courage and daring you showed in times of danger. I was particularly struck by your ability to travel through time.

Due to events which are presently threatening the kingdom which I serve and the well-being of its monarch, I humbly request that you accept this invitation to come and help me restore peace to the realm.

Captain Artashtah, who bears this letter, is equipped with all that is necessary to bring you to us.

Respectfully yours,
HARBONA
Grand Vizier and Head of Security.

P.S. The matter immediately concerns the safety of His Majesty and may involve an audience with him.

Judy's eyes were shining.

"Hey," I said to the stranger, who was standing with his arms folded and his sword grazing the floor, "where do you want to take us?"

He just stood there like a block of wood and said nothing.

"And anyway, Captain Artie, or however you say your name," added Judy, "how do we get there?"

The stranger liked this question, smiled and took the scroll from me. He spread it out on the floor and suddenly it turned into a sort of carpet. He sat on it and pulled at the fringes; it lifted off the floor, took a turn around the room, and landed again.

"Come on, then, let's go!" announced Judy, and jumped off her bed. "If we managed to deal with Antiochus and the whole Greek army during Hannukah, I'm sure we can handle what this Harbona wants us to do."

I ran to the closet and took out my Walkman and her Polaroid camera. This trip wasn't going to be like Hannukah when we flew through centuries of time in Star Dreidel and didn't have even one picture to prove that we hadn't made it all up.

I let Judy get on the carpet first and sat down behind her. The stranger smiled at us, took off his hat and began to talk into it.

"Good Evening," he began. "This is Captain Artashtah speaking. We shall be flying at a height of approximately seven thousand five hundred feet at an average speed of four hundred and fifty carpet miles per hour. Under the fringes of the craft you will find oxygen masks for use in emergencies. Please do not stretch out your hands or make any abrupt movements. Thank you, and have a pleasant flight."

The carpet shook a little, rose from the floor and drifted out the window.

We flew for miles. There was no moon that night and the carpet made no sound at all as it glided through the blackness. An hour after takeoff, we began to lose height. Below us appeared the lights of a huge city, not streetlamps but hundreds of blazing, sputtering torches. We flew down over a high wall that encircled the city and towards a huge palace with golden towers.

We could hear sounds of singing and dancing as we landed. "He's having another party," murmured the captain, and sighed as he helped us off the carpet. We followed Artashtah through a lot of fancy gardens that had little bridges over streams and pools. Cute, I thought. Luckily, Artashtah spoke up before I was tempted to explore it all on my own.

"Careful," he warned us as we crossed a bridge, "there are alligators in there."

Before we knew it, we were beside the palace. We all slipped through a small, hidden door and made our way through a maze of shadowy corridors. We turned and twisted and eventually, at the end of one especially long corridor, we saw a man with a limp coming towards us through the darkness.

"I am your host, Harbona," he explained as he kissed us on both cheeks. "I am honored that you have chosen to join me. Please come this way."

He led us into a little room and closed the door carefully. There was a bronze table piled high with fruit in the center of the room. I stretched out my hand for a plum, but Judy stepped very

Below us
appeared the lights of a huge city.

hard on my foot. I only just managed to turn a gasp of pain into a polite cough.

We sat down on mats on the floor.

"I regret that I must enter immediately upon the problem that has brought you to us," said Harbona. "Allow me to briefly outline what has transpired up to your arrival:

"1. Not long ago, a plot to assassinate His Majesty was exposed. Both the conspirators were caught and hanged.

"2. Then the King threw out the Queen — it is not important for you to know why — and a new Queen was chosen. We know nothing about this new Queen. She refuses to tell anyone anything. Unfortunately, we fear she may be an enemy agent.

"3. The King has something of a drinking habit. He is open, therefore, to being told all sorts of things by the wrong kind of people. He has just promoted one of these — here in the palace we call him the Aggagite — to the post of Minister of Defense.

"4. The Aggagite has access to all the most important people in the kingdom, and definitely has ideas above his station. We fear he may be planning a coup. We must have him watched."

I could see out of the corner of my eye that Artashtah was eating some of the fruit, so I took a couple of plums. Judy gave me one of her Looks, but I ignored it and, before sinking my teeth into one of the plums, asked Harbona how he thought we could help.

"These matters," he said solemnly, "are, of course, of the utmost delicacy. The Queen, while a mystery to all of us, is still the Queen for all that. I would not want to anger or insult her. She must be approached and observed discreetly. I have therefore arranged for Judy to be taken into the harem as a lady-in-waiting to the Queen. I leave it to your talents, Judy, to find favor with the Queen and to become her confidante."

"I'll do my best," Judy promised.

"You, Danny, must keep an eye on the Aggagite. It will not be easy. While many of us suspect the Aggagite, he enjoys the King's favor. He is a powerful and dangerous man. The best position I could obtain for you is as the babysitter for the Aggagite's youngest son. You will have to use all the ingenuity you possess to somehow free yourself from your duties as babysitter and get close to the Aggagite. I'm sorry that I could obtain no better placement for you."

Even though it seemed that I was going to be in a pretty difficult situation, I thought I should try to make Harbona feel better. He looked awfully troubled.

"Don't worry, Harbona," I reassured him. "You've done what you could—now it's up to us."

We shook hands on the deal. Then Harbona asked if there was anything he could do for us.

"Yes," Judy sighed. "Could we please go to bed? We're exhausted."

I didn't raise any objections — I couldn't. I was already falling asleep on the floor with a peach in each hand and my mouth full of plums.

Chapter Two

Into the City

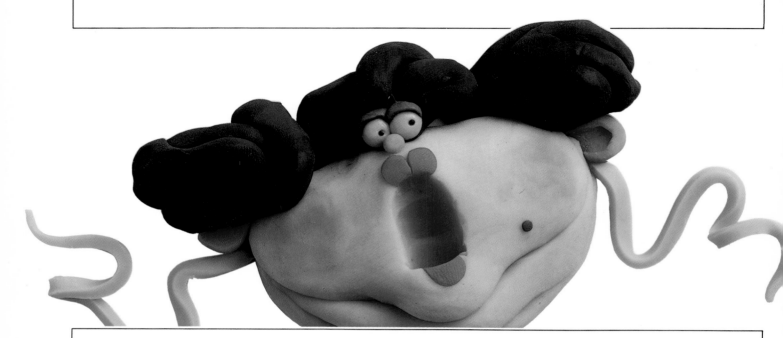

"He's awake, he's awake!"

I opened my eyes — and couldn't believe what I saw. Above me, there was a gold ceiling and around me were strange, arched windows. I was lying on a mattress on the floor and there was a figure shaking my elbow. It had a veil half covering its face and a long braid hung down its back.

And it had Judy's voice. But this could no way be my sister, who stages a four-act drama every time Mom tries to get her to braid her hair. Where was I??

"Come on! Get up, get dressed, let's get started," the figure continued.

I pinched myself. OW. Well, at least I was awake.

"He always takes forever to wake up," complained the voice. "Think! Plots at the Palace. The Aggagite. Harbona. Come on!"

I scrambled to my feet. How could I have forgotten?

Artashtah came into the room with a bundle of clothes. In five minutes flat I was in disguise too: sandals, silk shirt, baggy trousers, even an earring in one ear. I hid the Walkman under my shirt. Judy had already taken the Polaroid.

Outside the palace, a taxi was waiting to take me to the Aggagite. Harbona was standing next to it.

Believe me, riding 10 feet
above the ground on the back
of that camel was like a fairy tale.

Some taxi. Never before have I seen a taxi with two humps. Harbona told me to pass information to Artashtah who would be disguised as a fruit seller with a stand right outside the Aggagite's palace.

"If he's not there," continued Harbona, "then use the taxi." He lifted one of the camel's humps — it was completely hollow. "It's a homing camel — it knows to come straight back here."

I hiked myself up behind Artashtah and we started off.

Believe me, riding 10 feet above the ground on the back of that camel was like a fairy tale. The streets were packed with people greeting each other at the tops of their lungs, merchants selling their wares, and wandering musicians. Donkeys, camels and horses were everywhere. The air was a blur of color and full of the smell of sweet spices.

Artashtah stopped the camel outside a palace crowned with two silver domes. He spoke to a forbidding looking guard at the gate and we were taken to the palace courtyard. An old man dressed in very fine clothes stood waiting.

"The Aggagite?" I whispered to Artashtah.

He stifled a chuckle. "Karshton, the Aggagite's chamberlain," he explained.

"May it so please Your Honor," said Artashtah, "my master, Harbona, has sent this boy to serve in His Excellency the Aggagite's household as servant to his youngest son."

"Most kind," responded Karshton, "but how am I to know that this young boy is capable of filling the post?"

"I beg Your Honor to be assured that my master would not send a servant not capable of fulfilling this important task," I put in. What kind of talk was this, anyhow?

"Very well," said Karshton. "Boy, follow me."

I shook hands with Artashtah and realized that he was passing me something. It was a gold coin. "For emergencies," he whispered.

Karshton grabbed me and dragged me inside. The doors clanged shut behind me. I was in the Aggagite's palace.

Chapter Three

Death and Destruction

The Aggagite's son's room was enormous — I wish ours was half as big. In one corner was a sort of bed. Karshton told me to make it up while he went to get the lady of the house to have a look at me.

Some bed. I don't think I've ever seen so many sheets, blankets and pillows. It's a good thing Mom wasn't there. At home I never make beds, on principle.

I peeked out the window, and the first thing I saw was Artashtah, selling fruit across the way. He gave me a friendly wave. I waved back and began to feel better. And then there was a voice behind me.

"So we wave instead of work, do we?"

It was the Aggagite's wife, short, fat and ugly. It didn't take me long to decide that I hated her. She marched over to the bed and pulled all my work on to the floor in a heap.

"We don't make them like that here," she screeched. "What's more, we work. We don't wave. Do you understand?" She boxed my ears hard and left.

A whistle came from the street. I looked out and saw Artashtah pointing at a tall man with seven guards entering the palace. The man I had to trail! But how?

That second Karshton came running in.

"Come," he panted, and began to pull me out the door.

"Why?" I demanded. I was getting sick and tired of being pushed around.

"All the servants are ill," explained Karshton. "They have been eating fruit sold by that new man opposite. You will have to pour the wine for His Excellency. He is having guests to dinner."

Artashtah would make a great crook. He thinks of everything.

At the dining hall, I had to stand behind two enormous wine jugs and pour wine every time I saw an empty cup. My position was perfect for hearing everything that was said.

The Aggagite sat down and began shouting.

"Everybody, but everybody bows to me!" he fumed. "But he just stands there and doesn't bat an eye!"

"Disgraceful," agreed his wife with her mouth full. "But I may have an idea . . ."

"Yes?" demanded the Aggagite, a nasty light in his eyes.

"Not in front of the servants, darling," she cooed. "You. Out."

That was all I needed. To leave just as things were getting interesting.

Luckily, I remembered the Walkman. I took it out from under my shirt, pressed the 'record' button and stood it behind one of the wine jugs. Then I ran out before that woman took it into her head to start beating me up again.

I slowly made my way to the dining-hall after all the torches had been put out. There was the Walkman. Now all I had to do was send it to Harbona.

I decided to let Artashtah take it to Harbona. As I began to cross the courtyard to his fruit stand my feet suddenly left the ground.

I was on the end of a huge arm. The night watchman!

"Where are you off to, my young friend?" he bellowed. "Don't you know that anyone running around at this time of night is executed?"

"No . . . I didn't know . . . I'm sorry . . ." I babbled. "I only came out to buy a peach. I can't sleep if I don't have one . . ."

I know it was a dumb thing to say. I guess the night watchman thought so too, because he took out his sword and began to sharpen it on a stone.

"After an execution we take the head to the Master and are rewarded with a silver coin," he said happily.

I remembered the gold coin. "Have this," I offered, pulling it out of my pocket, "and please let me go."

The watchman took the coin and a slow smile spread over his face.

"Very good!" He laughed. "Now I get a gold coin and a silver one. Start praying, boy." He grunted as he droppped the coin in his pocket and raised the sword.

Luckily, I remembered the Walkman.

I closed my eyes and waited to die. And waited. After a little bit, I figured that maybe dying wasn't so painful after all. I opened my eyes. The watchman was stretched unconscious on the ground and behind him stood . . . Judy!

"Wh . . . wha . . . what are you doing here?" I stammered.

"Harbona brought me to see the Aggagite's palace tonight," she replied. "Artashtah had just lifted me over the wall when I saw that lout. Harbona gave me a handkerchief with some knockout drops on it. I got behind the watchman and . . . well, you can see for yourself what happened next."

Generally speaking, I don't thank sisters. I mean, what is there to thank them for? But this time I hugged Judy like I really meant it. I realized she was trembling too.

"Tell Harbona to get me to the palace tomorrow," I told her. "I've got some information for him."

"Fine," said Judy. She ran for the wall. Artashtah lowered a rope; she shinnied up it and disappeared.

That night I slept like the dead — well, almost.

In the morning, Karshton woke me with a kick. "Go and collect the Master's son. He's at a party at the King's palace with Harbona. Make sure you bring him back safely."

Harbona was waiting for me at the door of his secret room. Judy was already there. From the expression on her face, I knew she had news for him, too: but I bet it wasn't as good as mine. I pressed the 'play' button on the Walkman. Harbona nearly passed out when he heard it; but the Aggagite's voice made him pull himself together. It seemed very little could disturb him for long.

I hate to admit this. It was a lousy recording. All we could hear was voice after voice saying, "The King . . . death . . . decree . . . the 13th . . . kill . . . destruction . . . the King."

"Enough," said Harbona. "This confirms all my suspicions. First Bagtan and Teresh, and now the Aggagite. But I doubt that the King will take my word for this. I must have further proof."

"There's one more thing," I said. "There's one man at the city gate who won't bow to the Aggagite, and it makes him mad."

"Mmm," said Harbona thoughtfully. "And who is this man?"

"I don't know," I admitted. "That was when they ordered me out."

"Very well," said Harbona. "The next part of your mission is to find out who this man is. The Aggagite's son will be kept occupied for a little longer and you can start work straight away. You have my sincerest thanks, Danny, for your brave work thus far. Now, Judy, what have you been able to find out?"

"The Queen liked me right away," she said proudly. "She's the most beautiful woman in the kingdom, maybe the world. There was a beauty contest with a hundred and twenty-seven candidates to find the new queen and she won hands down. The other ladies-in-waiting say the competition was tough, too.

"The information that I have is that a mysterious man visits the Queen from time to time. He arrived just now while I was sitting with her. She ordered me straight out of the room, but I listened at the door and I heard him telling her not to give away her background just yet. She agreed. Then you called for me to bring me here.

"I like her, though. I don't think she could be a spy."

"We cannot be sure just yet, Judy," Harbona said quietly. "We must be certain. You each have a new mission. Danny, you must find the man who will not bow to the Aggagite. Judy, please return to the harem and, if possible, follow the Queen's mysterious visitor. I must know who he is. I wish you both success — and safety."

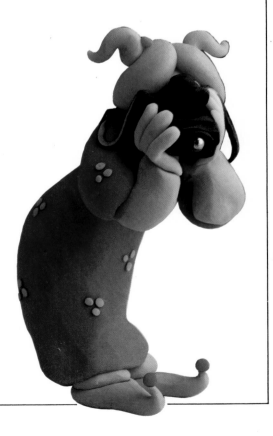

Chapter Four

The Mix Up

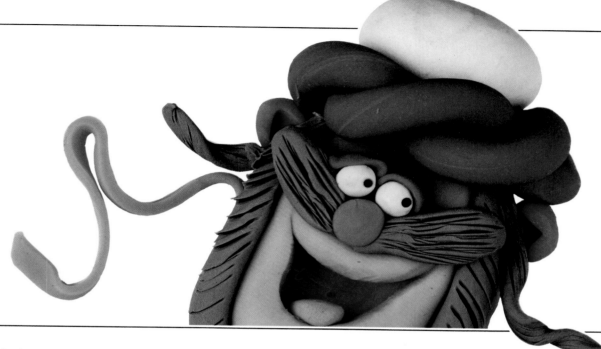

Judy went back to the harem. Before I left, I took a peek into a huge silver tent which had been set up on the lawn. It was full of children who were watching some dumb puppet show, and there in the front row was the boy I had to look after. I recognized him at once. He was the image of his mother.

Artashtah was waiting for me with the taxi, Camel #009, outside the palace gate. It was just like a carnival: merchants were selling all sorts of things I'd never seen in my life and there were crowds of people pushing, shoving and complaining that it was their turn to see the King, they'd been there for days and what was the country coming to, anyhow? The next thing I know, my eardrums are nearly blown out by a blast of trumpets.

"His Excellency the Aggagite!" yelled a servant.

He swept up to the gate with his nose in the air. Everyone fell to their knees and began to rub their noses in the dust. As he passed me, I ducked down behind the camel. Good. He hadn't noticed me. And then I realized why. One man wasn't bowing.

The Aggagite pushed his face up under the man's nose. The man just stared straight ahead. I made my way through the crowd. This had to be him.

"My good ben Yair ben Shimei ben Kish the Yemenite," spat the Aggagite, "you don't appear to be bowing."

"So it would seem, Your Excellency," ben Yair agreed.

"There's a nasty surprise in store for you, you proud idiot," the Aggagite screamed, "and for your precious people."

"He who laughs last, laughs longest," observed ben Yair.

The Aggagite swung around furiously and continued on his way. The crowd slowly rose to their feet and stared at ben Yair in terrified curiousity.

"So this is the man who gets him so uptight," I said to Artashtah. "We'd better follow him."

The crowd was beginning to break up and ben Yair also turned to go.

"He's going towards the Jewish Quarter," whispered Artashtah. It was easy to keep him in sight from the high back of Camel #009.

We must have gone about fifty yards when I had a strange sensation that someone was behind us. We went on for a few paces and then turned again. Just as I thought. We were being trailed too!

"I think it's time for a little surprise," I said to Artashtah, who nodded.

When ben Yair turned down a side street, we followed but stopped just after the corner. Artashtah threw open the camel's hump, pulled out a cord and threw it to me. We stretched it between us across the street and waited. A few seconds later, a hooded figure came running down the street, tripped over the cord and fell head over heels. Together, we bundled it into the hump and slammed down the lid. Then we set off again after ben Yair. Just as Artashtah had predicted, he turned off into the Jewish Quarter. Mission accomplished. We knew where he lived.

We hurried back to the palace, where Harbona was trying hard not to look impatient. You had to admire his cool.

"Have we got news!" I could hardly breathe, I was so excited. "We know who the Aggagite hates and we caught someone trailing us as well!"

Harbona was going to love this, I thought as I whipped open the camel's trick hump and hauled out our prisoner. Artashtah ripped away the hood.

And there in front of us stood … Judy. And she wasn't looking too happy, if you get what I mean.

"But…but…" I began.

"But nothing!" she shrieked. "Is this the thanks I get for saving your life last night? Come here, you…"

"Hey," I said from behind Harbona, "who told you to trail us anyhow?"

"Why would I want to trail you? I don't trail idiots! I was trailing the Queen's visitor!"

"The heck you were!" I bellowed back. "You were trailing us and we were trailing the man who wouldn't bow to the Aggagite — Mr. ben Yair. Can't you mind your own business just for once?"

"I was! I was trailing the Queen's visitor!"

"Excuse me," I said, "but that was the man who wouldn't bow!"

" Excuse me, honored guests," put in Harbona, "but he would appear, would he not, to be the same man. Did you notice, Danny, if they called him 'the Yemenite'?"

I nodded.

"I know him," Harbona mused. "He is a Jew and an important minister. In fact, it was he who exposed the last plot to assassinate the King. A good man. It is no surprise that the Aggagite does not like him."

"Pardon the interruption, Master Harbona," began Artashtah, "but the puppet show is over and Danny has to get the Aggagite's son home before anyone becomes suspicious."

"You are quite right," agreed Harbona. "Very well then: Danny, now we must find out who the Aggagite is plotting to destroy. Judy, find out what the Queen has been discussing with Mr. ben Yair. I think we may be well on the way to solving this mystery. Be cautious, my young friends."

Chapter Five

Danny in Danger

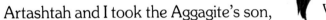

Artashtah and I took the Aggagite's son, 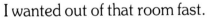 Vizata, home.

When we got back, we were going to play soccer, but when I saw them using a skull for a ball I said I didn't feel so well. Then Vizata took me to his room to see his collection of snakes. As he wound three big cobras around his neck, he told me I'd have to do the same.

"But not with these," he said. "These aren't poisonous. The ones over there are, and they're the ones for you."

I wanted out of that room fast.

Suddenly, I heard Karshton in the hall telling the servants to "ready a feast." I had to listen in.

"Hey, Vizata," I said. "How about a game of hide and go seek? You count to a hundred and I'll hide."

He forgot the snakes and began counting. I took off for the dining-hall and hid behind one of the wine jugs.

The Aggagite was standing at the head of the table with a delighted expression on his face.

"My lords, gentlemen and wife Zeresh," he said, "I have the King's official permission to massacre the Jews!"

They gave a huge cheer and my knees began to shake.

"I told the silly fool," the Aggagite continued, beaming, "how rich they are and how snobby they are about keeping themselves apart from us. I told him he could have all their money and an extra sum from me if he'd let me clear up the matter myself."

"And I suppose the sap agreed," said Zeresh.

"Of course," leered her husband. "So the thirteenth is the day. And I want to deal with that ben Yair ben Shimei ben Kish personally."

Zeresh gave him a round of applause.

Then I heard a familiar voice whinning behind me. "I found you, I found you!" And there was that little creep Vizata pointing straight at me.

Zeresh personally gave two guards a hand to pull me out. "Aha," she said. "A small spy, I think. I didn't like this one from the first moment I set eyes on him."

"How did he get in here?" asked one of the guests.

"Harbona sent him, sir," replied Karshton, who had gone very pale.

"Now what??" demanded the Aggagite.

"Easy, darling," said Zeresh. "We'll give the dear boy a little time to think about the world before leaving it, I think. Don't you?"

"Excellent," said her husband.

Within ten minutes, my hands and feet were tied and I was in a cold, dark cell. I couldn't believe it. Two huge guards passed the door every ten minutes or so to look in. As far as I was concerned, this was one story that wasn't going to have a happy ending.

Slowly, the time went by. The only light I had was when one of the guards opened the door from time to time to check on me.

And then I remembered. The Walkman. It was still under my shirt. I began to twist and turn. The Walkman fell to the floor. I waited for the guards to look in one more time, and as they locked the door again I managed to press the 'record' button. I spoke into the machine, trying to disguise my voice as much as I could.

When the door opened next, I began to yell like a maniac.

"Save me!!" I shrieked. "Help! Please save me! There are demons in here! They're speaking to me! Help!!!" And so on.

"What's all the noise for?" one of the guards demanded. "Shut your mouth."

I was in a cold, dark cell.

"That black box is talking, it has demons in it, oh help!" I screamed.

I was beginning to enjoy myself.

Behind my back, I pressed the 'play' button and gave the Walkman to the guard. Suddenly it began to speak.

"Give ear, O Guards!" I was really pretty satisfied with the way it sounded. "I am The Destroyer, King of the Demons!"

The guard began to scream and his companion clapped both hands over his mouth.

"I command you," my voice continued, "to release this child. Take him to where the camels are parked!"

They untied me and we raced to the camel parking lot.

"Put him upon the beast at which he points," continued the Walkman, "and close your eyes."

They put me on top of Camel #009 and shut their eyes. I jumped into the hollow hump and pulled the lid down after me.

I guess they opened their eyes at some point and didn't see me because I heard cries of "demons, demons!" and the sound of running feet. I jumped out of the hump, untied the camel and let it take me to Harbona.

Even though it was about midnight when I arrived at the King's palace, there was a large crowd outside the gate. They were watching a man who was standing in front of it. He was crying and yelling like a lunatic. At first I thought he was just crazy; but then I realized that everybody was listening to him. The guards weren't arresting him, people weren't laughing.

He seemed familiar. I stopped the camel and stood on tiptoe on one of the humps to get a better look, which wasn't easy. The torches were so bright I could see everything.

I knew him. . . of course I knew him! It was ben Yair, the Queen's mysterious friend. He was full of surprises. Harbona had to hear about this. Camel #009 knew its stuff and within seconds I burst into Harbona's room. Judy was with him and I quickly told them everything.

Judy thought she should see the Queen and Harbona agreed. She ran off. In a short time she came back with a bundle of clothes and we ran together to the gate. We pushed through the crowd and held out the bundle to ben Yair.

"It is the Queen's wish that you wear these clothes and take off your mourning garb," Judy said softly.

Ben Yair looked at her.

"Return to your Queen and tell her that I shall not cease to mourn until she ensures this dreadful decree is revoked," he answered. "It is my duty to weep and wail until the conscience of the good people in this kingdom is awakened."

"But it is the Queen's command," said Judy.

"Return to your mistress and take the clothes with you," he replied.

We had no choice. We returned to the palace. Judy disappeared into the harem, which gave me some time to get my breath back and think things through. The order to slaughter the Jews must have been made public. If it had, what should we do?

We went back to the palace gate.

"The Queen wishes to know why you are in mourning!" Judy shouted over the crowd.

Ben Yair told Judy about the terrible order to which the King had agreed.

"The Queen must convince her husband to revoke this decree and save us from Haman ben Hamdata the Aggagite's evil hand," he finished.

"Haman," murmured Judy, nodding to herself.

When we told the Queen of the decree and of ben Yair's demand, she told us to tell him that if anyone went into the King's throne room uninvited they would be executed. Her included.

We took the Queen's answer to ben Yair.

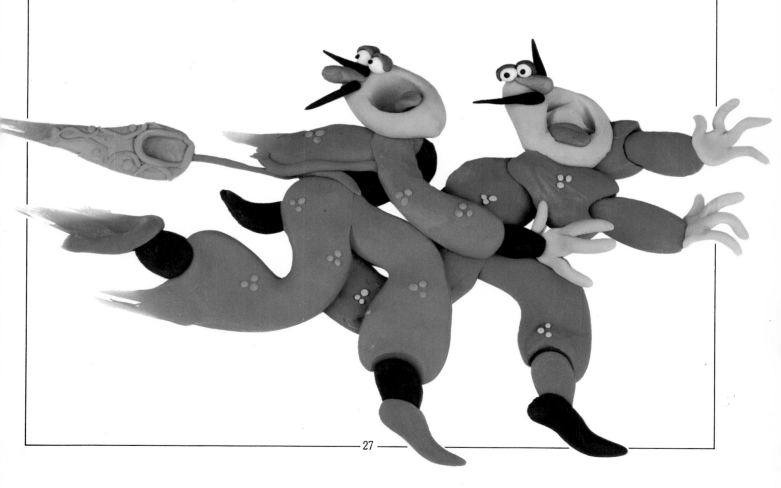

They were watching a man who was standing in front of the palace. He was crying and yelling like a lunatic.

"It will be no safer for the Queen in the King's house if she says nothing," he replied. "Risking her life is the only way she has any possibility of saving herself and her people."

We went to the Queen. Her next message made us proud of her courage.

"The Queen will see the King," Judy announced. "She asks that you and all of the Jews fast and pray that she will leave his presence alive."

Ben Yair nodded his head and left the square.

When we got back to the palace, we found the Queen crying. Judy ran to her and hugged her tightly.

"Hadassah, don't cry," Judy said. "It will be all right."

The Queen looked at Judy in astonishment.

"How do you know my name?" she whispered.

"I know that Hadassah is your Hebrew name though everyone knows you by the Persian name of Esther; that Mr. ben Yair is your uncle and that his first name is Mordechai; and that you have told no one that you are a Jew. Please don't worry. My brother and I will help you. And I know that you will be all right."

Hadassah/Esther shook her head in speechless wonder.

They walked off together to her rooms.

My head was spinning. I staggered off to find Harbona, but he wasn't in his room, and I curled up on the floor there and fell asleep.

Chapter Six

Who Dares to Enter

Harbona came and woke me at noon. Judy had told him the whole story and he wanted to help. We were to see His Majesty himself right away.

So, Judy, Harbona and I went to see the King. I have to say I was a bit nervous —after all, you don't meet kings every day, do you? We passed through endless corridors and eventually came to a silk curtain. Behind this was a long marble entrance hall, and behind that was the King's throne room.

It was tremendous —all arches and statues. His throne stood between two golden lions. The King himself was looking a little nervous and red in the face.

"Harbona!" he roared as we came in, "who are these two strangers?"

"Greetings to Your Majesty," said Harbona soothingly. "May I introduce Danny and Judy, two children who have travelled through time to meet you."

We bowed low before him.

"How about a drink?" he offered.

And just then, there was the noise of someone coming through the courtyard. The sentries at the door stood sharply to attention and shouldered their spears. I suddenly felt cold all over. The King went pale and hid behind his throne.

"Someone is coming into the throne room uninvited," whispered Harbona. "How could anyone be so foolish?"

I had to see who it was. I made my way quietly to the sentry post.

Oh no.

I ran back to Harbona.

"It's… it's… it's…"

"Who??" asked Harbona and Judy in chorus.

"E…e…e…"

"WHO IS IT?" hollered Harbona. I'd never heard him shout before.

"Esther," I whispered. "The Queen is coming."

"What shall we do?" murmured Harbona.

I couldn't think of anything. I knew that the second the Queen set foot in the throne room she would lose her life. The strangest thing of all at that moment was the way Judy was acting. She said confidently, "Nothing will happen. The King will just let her in."

"I have grave doubts, Judy," said Harbona.

"I'm perfectly sure," she said tranquilly.

She may have been, but I wasn't. Especially when five guards ran at Esther and grabbed her.

One put a spear to her throat. The King crawled out from behind his throne, grabbed his scepter and lifted it in the air.

"If he lowers it completely," whispered Harbona, "she will die. If he extends it towards her, she lives."

I could hear my heart beating. The room had become completely still. Finally, like a miracle, the King extended the scepter to Esther.

The guards released her and she bowed low before the King.

"You should really ask before you come to see me, my dear," said the King indulgently. "What is your request?"

And then, she invited the King to a party that night! I couldn't believe it! The Jews faced the possibility of being wiped out,   and Esther was talking about   parties???

"I have invited Haman too, my lord," she added.

"Oh?" said the King. "Why?"

"I should so much like for him to be there," Esther said simply.

"Very well, then, my dear," said the King. "But you will make sure the place is well guarded, won't you? I don't want any attempts made on my life."

"May I suggest, my lord, that your honored guests and your vizier, Harbona, be present in an adjacent room?" said Esther. "Though I ask Your Majesty not to tell Haman of this, as he believes this honor is for him alone."

The King scowled.

"I'm beginning to get a little tired of this Haman," he confided to Harbona in a loud whisper.

"Really, Your Majesty?" said Harbona.

"Well, I must make myself ready," said the King. "Harbona, you can stay and help me dress. How about a drink?"

Judy and I bowed hastily and left. I'm sure I saw Esther wink at us as we went out.

Judy and I went back to Harbona's room. Artashtah had chicken, fruit and sweets ready for us to eat. If I thought about it, I was starving. But the only thing I could think about was how Judy could be so sure about everything. I could hardly contain myself.

"How did you know?" I demanded. "How did you know nothing would happen to Esther?"

"How did I know?" Judy swallowed a mouthful of chicken. "Do you remember that I was reading the story of Esther the night we came here?"

"So?"

"What do you mean, 'So'?" asked Judy. "It's all in there. Think about it. Haman, Mordechai, Esther, Harbona. . . we're in Ahasuerus's kingdom. We must be in Shushan, in Persia. We're in the story of Purim!"

"Okay. Maybe you're right, but. . ."

"Maybe!" said Judy indignantly.

"Maybe. Probably! Definitely! But Queen Esther still hasn't said anything to the King about the decree to kill all the Jews, and as long as that stands we're still in big trouble."

"Danny, I'm telling you, Esther is going to get us out of this. You'll see."

I shook my head in exasperation as I piled my plate high with food. She was probably right, but I wasn't going to relax until that decree was revoked. And as far as I could see, it would take a lot more than a party to do that.

Esther's party was my first for adults only, and I didn't even mind that Judy, Harbona and I had to be in the room next door. Esther made sure we had all kinds of sweets and a drink called nectar. We could hear everything, all the music and the dancing. There was only a curtain between our room and the party so we could see what was going on if we had to. Esther was dancing a lot with Haman, and the King wasn't liking it much, I can tell you. He was certainly drinking a lot.

Chapter Seven

The King's Delight

Though the party at bottom was a pretty serious thing, I was having the time of my life. Even Harbona spent the whole time tapping his good foot to the music and told us about the King's parties of days gone by. Apparently, there had been one that ran for one hundred and eighty days! Half a year! Too bad they don't do things like that any more.

And then we heard voices. Someone was standing right by the curtain. I took a peek. There was the King, with Esther.

"Tell me, sweetheart," he said, and his voice sounded tight, "why are you dancing so much with Haman?"

"Haman is an important man, my lord," Esther replied. "I find him most brave and talented. He is so near to being the King that it is almost as good as dancing with you."

"Haman," muttered the King. "Haman, Haman, it's all I ever hear these days."

Harbona was obviously pleased by the turn of the conversation.

"Please do not distress yourself, my lord," said Esther, smiling very sweetly at him. "He is so very charming…and he has told me that when he becomes King, he will…"

"When he becomes King?" Ahasuerus glared.

"I am sure he only said it in jest, my lord." Esther acted, as if she didn't notice his anger. "How are you enjoying my party? Would it please you to come to another tomorrow?"

I thought the King would explode.

"Let me think, my dear," he said with difficulty. "I shall announce it myself if I agree."

Esther smiled at him and went off to find Haman, who was strutting around in front of a mirror practicing how to draw his sword without getting it stuck. The King took a stiff drink. Then he walked unsteadily to the middle of the room and announced, "I do hereby invite Haman ben Hamdata the Aggagite to be present at a party to be held here by the Queen and myself tomorrow night at sundown."

Haman actually flushed with pleasure. "So kind," he simpered, and kissed Esther's hand rather wetly. Then he bowed and left for his palace.

The party wound down after that. We began to go to our room, and the King to his; but just as we were going, he called us back.

"Listen, my dear children," he told us, "I am surrounded by dangerous men who are plotting against my life. Perhaps you can suggest how I might protect myself?"

I thought of an electric fence, and then realized that electricity hadn't been invented yet. Then Judy had a great idea.

"If you were to take a lot of rattles," she suggested, "and tie them all together, you could string them around the yard or across the door of your bedroom. Then, if anyone tried to attack you, they'd trip over the cord and you'd hear them."

"You are a genius," declared the King, and kissed her on the forehead. Harbona says that this is a great honor, but I'm still glad it wasn't me.

He sent Harbona off to find some rattles immediately. We said good night again and went off to bed, thinking that the evening was finally over.

We couldn't have been more wrong.

We were just falling asleep when Harbona knocked at the door. The King couldn't sleep and was asking for us. We went, of course.

"Thought you might like to hear my diary," the King said wearily. "Good story in it about how they tried to kill me last time."

A servant brought the diary and began to read. What had happened the last time was that two men, Bagtan and Teresh, had tried to poison the King, but they'd been overheard by Mordechai and hanged.

"How did I reward him?" demanded the King.

The servant checked the list in the back of the diary but couldn't find any record of a reward. "Disgraceful!" muttered the King. "I must reward Mordechai."

And then, suddenly, there was a clatter of rattles outside.

"Spies!" the King screamed, and ran out into the yard. We followed him.

It was Haman with a team of eight men. They were struggling to carry a huge tree. When they saw the King, they dropped the tree and immediately stood to attention.

"What are you doing sneaking around at this time of night?" demanded the King.

"Um… Well, Your Majesty…" Haman stammered, "I thought this tree would make an excellent gallows for that Jew, Mordechai. When we kill all the Jews, that is. . .you do remember the decree about the Jews, I hope, Your Majesty?"

The King stroked his beard thoughtfully. Judy and I held our breath.

"Well, Haman," he finally said, "now that you're here, you might as well tell me the best way to reward a man who has supported and aided me in many ways. How would you reward such a man?"

The King couldn't sleep

A crafty look came to Haman's face.

A crafty look came to Haman's face. Naturally, he said, he was delighted to have been chosen to advise His Most Esteemed Majesty. It seemed to him that if the King were to dress this man — whoever he was — in royal clothes and put him on a white horse and have some good-for-nothing — say that Mordechai — lead him around the city crying, "This shall be done to the man whom the King delights to honor," well, that would do very nicely, he thought.

"Excellent," said the King. "You are just the man."

"I knew it all along, Your Majesty, sir," said Haman. "Shall I call for Mordechai and tell him to get a horse ready?"

"This minute," said the King. "Except that, of course, Mordechai will ride the horse and you will lead it. See to it, would you?"

"But . . . but . . ."

"No buts, my dear sir. At once!"

Haman's face dissolved in hatred and frustration, but there was nothing he could do. As he stumbled out of the courtyard, I think he must have recognized me: his face turned an interesting shade of green.

"This-shall-be-done-to-the-man-
whom-the-king-delights-to-honor."

Because the King wanted it done immediately, the whole city had to be awakened. A servant was sent to fetch Mordechai, who was dressed in the King's second-best suit (he was saving the best one for the party, he explained) and put on the horse. The army was sent down the street blowing trumpets in case anyone had managed to stay asleep. Haman followed trying to hide his face, leading Mordechai and muttering, "This shall be done to the man whom the King delights to honor."

"I can't hear you, ben Hamdata!" bellowed the King.

''THIS·SHALL·BE·DONE·TO·THE·MAN·WHOM·THE·KING·DELIGHTS·TO·HONOR,''

bawled Haman furiously.

The crowd pelted Haman with orange peels and raw eggs, which didn't improve his temper at all.

The best part happened as the procession passed Haman's palace. There in the window were Zeresh and Vizata.

"My Father's on the horse; my Father's on the horse!" sang Vizata.

"Yes, and Mordechai is leading him!" shouted Zeresh. "Mordechai! A present from me to you! One…two…three…" and she threw down a bucket of filthy liquid, straight on Haman's head.

Judy and I laughed louder than anyone. We knew whose head the gunk had landed on.

Chapter Eight

The Final Curtain

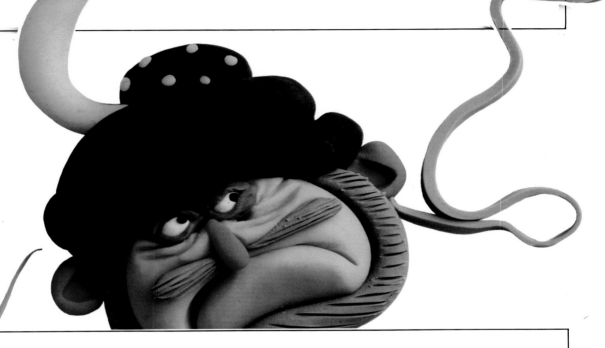

The next evening, Esther had her second party. Only Haman and the King were there with her; Harbona, Judy and I were next door again. Esther carried on dancing with Haman, and the King got even angrier than he had been the night before. I noticed that he wasn't drinking much at all.

He marched up to Haman and Esther in the middle of a dance and pulled the Queen roughly away into a corner.

"What are you doing?" he demanded. "Why do you have to keep dancing with that man? You know how angry it makes me!"

"Ah," said Esther. "My lord, he has been making me promises."

"Promises?" said the King. "I see. Well, then, we'll see who can promise you the most. I'll start. You can have anything you want, even half of my kingdom. There!"

"Anything?" asked Esther, and she sounded serious.

"Anything!" declared the King. "You are my dear wife, and you have my royal word as my bond."

Esther fell to her knees and kissed the hem of the King's robe.

"My lord," she said, "I ask you for my life." Her eyes were full of tears.

"Esther," said the King bewildered, "what do you mean?"

"My lord," she continued, "I make this request for all of my people as well as myself. Let Your Majesty know that one man intends to destroy my people, and me also."

and there was Haman
kissing her hands.

The King was astounded.

"My Queen," he murmured, "what people are you from?"

"I am a Jew, my lord," answered Esther.

"Who would destroy you?" asked the King. Esther rose to her feet.

"This is the man!" she cried, pointing straight at Haman.

"This is treason of the highest order," mused the King. Haman had gone completely white.

"I shall retire to the garden," continued the King. "I do not wish to be disturbed."

He turned on his heel and left the room.

Haman suddenly exploded into action. He burst through the door of the room where we were sitting.

"Harbona," he shrieked, "save me from this fool of a King!"

"Fool?" said Harbona, and turned his back on him.

Haman grabbed me by the shoulders.

"Save me, my child," he pleaded. "I always liked you."

"I suppose that's why you agreed to put me in prison?" I asked him.

He threw me aside and ran back into the Queen's room. Esther had fallen to the couch, exhausted. Haman knelt beside her and began kissing her hands frantically.

"Save me! Oh, Queen, save me, save me!" he pleaded.

At that very moment the King came back. I could imagine what was going through his mind. There was the Queen on the couch, and there was Haman kissing her hands.

"Vile traitor!" he roared. "It is not enough that you plot to kill my loyal subjects, but you

would steal my wife and assassinate me! Guards, hang him! Hang his whole family! Blot out his name forever!"

Harbona whispered something in the King's ear.

"Let it be as Harbona advises. The gallows you planned for the innocent shall be your own!"

The decree to massacre the Jews was overruled and Mordechai took over Haman's post. Judy and I didn't stay in Shushan to see what happened after that. We said a long goodbye to Harbona, Esther, Mordechai and the King. It wasn't easy, especially for Judy and Esther who had become such good friends. Finally, Artashtah unrolled the magic carpet and we were off.

Just before dawn, we flew through our window. Captain Artashtah repaired the broken pane with a few magic words. Then he had to go. This was hard for me — he'd been a brave friend, after all. Then he was gone and we curled up to sleep.

The next day, it felt as if we had dreamt the whole thing. Those goofy guards still had my Walkman, but on the floor by Judy's bed was a little pile of photographs. We looked at them together. There was a picture of Haman kissing the Queen's hand and another one of me in my disguise. There was one of Harbona standing smiling by the palace gate. And Judy had taken two or three of Esther. She really is very beautiful, and I don't often say that about girls, believe me.

Judy has a wooden box with a key, where she keeps all her private stuff so I can't get to it. She put the photos in that and locked the box tightly. I checked it just to make sure.

That night, after we'd finished our homework, we dressed up in costumes and the whole family read the Megillah from end to end. We ate Hamentaschen and shouted and sang and waved groggers. It was wonderful.

Just as Dad was beginning to look at the clock in that way he has when it's time for bed, Grandpa asked us if we had anything to tell him.

"Yes," we said together, and told them the whole story.

Then, of course, Grandma started whispering to Mom about how vivid our imaginations were, and was it something we'd eaten, and Grandpa chuckled about how we should take him along the next time because he'd always wanted to meet Bar Kochba.

"So you don't believe us?" smiled Judy. "Well, Danny and I have a little surprise for you."

She brought the wooden box, took the key from the string around her neck and opened it.

A small, white puff of smoke came from the box. The adults became very quiet. Judy turned the box upside down. There was all her private stuff. . .but the photographs had vanished. The family began to look at us as if we were crazy, particularly when I checked the box all over with my magnifying glass. Nothing. Well, okay, there was a little film of gold dust on the bottom, but that wasn't enough to convince anybody.

Judy and I looked at each other.

"Let's go to bed," she said sadly.

I agreed. You can bet the family really thought we were out of our minds when they heard that.

In our room, Judy told me that she hadn't taken the key from around her neck all day. And I believe her. Maybe it was Harbona; though I still can't figure out how he could do it without our seeing him.

So we didn't have any proof. What we did have were some great stories. I'd written up Grandpa's memories and Judy . . .well, she'd found her heroine.

The End

The Animated

HOLYDAYS

The Animated Haggadah (Pesach)
book and video
The Animated Menorah (Hannukah)
book and Hannukit
The Animated Megillah (Purim)

available soon:
The Animated Israel
(Israeli Independence Day)